P9-DJL-276

THE IMAGINARY OKAPI

Adapted by Judy Katschke
from the episode "The Imaginary Okapi" written by John Loy
for the series developed for television by Ford Riley

Illustrated by Francesco Legramandi and Gabriella Matta

A GOLDEN BOOK • NEW YORK

Copyright © 2017 Disney Enterprises, Inc. All rights reserved. Published in the United States by
Golden Books, an imprint of Random House Children's Books, a division of Penguin Random House LLC,
1745 Broadway, New York, NY 10019, and in Canada by Penguin Random House Canada Limited, Toronto,
in conjunction with Disney Enterprises, Inc. Golden Books, A Golden Book, A Little Golden Book, the
G colophon, and the distinctive gold spine are registered trademarks of Penguin Random House LLC.
randomhousekids.com
ISBN 978-0-7364-3719-6 (trade) — ISBN 978-0-7364-3720-2 (ebook)
Printed in the United States of America
10 9 8 7 6 5 4 3 2 1

Playing hide-and-seek is a great way for the members of the Lion Guard to practice their tracking skills. It's also a lot of fun!

"Gotcha!" Kion the lion shouts when he finds Fuli. "Now it's your turn to be 'it.' Close your eyes so we can all hide."

"Okay, but I warn you—I'm the fastest finder in the Pride Lands!" the cheetah says with a smile.

The search for hiding places is on! Kion, Bunga the honey badger, and Ono the egret quickly head off in different directions. Beshte moves a bit slower. Finding a hippo-sized hiding spot is never easy.

Soon Beshte settles himself behind a thick patch of bushes. But he is not alone. . . .

"Excuse me," says a soft voice.

Beshte looks this way and that. "Who said that? Who's there?" he asks.

An animal's head pops up. He has a long neck, a colorful face, and large ears. "I'm Ajabu," he says shyly.

Beshte has never seen an animal like Ajabu before. "Are you a zebra?" he asks. "Or a giraffe?"

"Neither," Ajabu laughs. "I'm an okapi!"

Ajabu is not from the Pride Lands. He was chased out of his home by a leopard.

Beshte gulps. Being chased is no fun—unless you're playing tag!

"We don't have any leopards in the Pride Lands. Hippo's honor," Beshte promises. He offers to give the timid okapi a tour of the area.

Meanwhile, the game of hide-and-seek is still going strong. Fuli sniffs out Bunga inside a hollow log. Next, she finds a trail of lion cub paw prints. Fuli is sure she is about to find Kion . . . but then she notices bigger, strange-looking tracks next to the paw prints.

"Game's over!" Fuli shouts. "You guys need to see this!"

Kion and Ono come out of hiding to check out the strange prints.

"These are leopard tracks!" Kion declares.

"Leopards don't live in the Pride Lands," Ono insists.

"There's one here now," Kion says, looking around. "The question is . . . where?"

Ono flies sky-high in search of the leopard. Before long, he sees a spotted cat at the gazelles' watering hole.

Ono flies back to his friends. "I saw the leopard!" he shouts. "He's going after some gazelles!"

"Lead the way," Kion says.

Back at the gazelles' watering hole, the leopard stalks his peaceful prey. But just as he is about to pounce . . .

"Get out of the Pride Lands, leopard—now!" Kion growls.

The leopard sees the Lion Guard and snarls. "The name's Makucha," he says, "and if you want me to go, you'll have to catch me!" Then he turns and races off.

The Lion Guard runs after Makucha. Fuli takes
the lead, chasing the leopard along a wide crevasse.
"You've got nowhere to go now!" Fuli shouts.
"That's what you think, cheetah!" Makucha snaps.
He leaps over the crevasse and runs away, laughing.

The Guard goes to find Beshte. The hippo is excited
to tell his friends about his new pal.

"His top half is like a giraffe, his bottom half looks like
a zebra, and his face looks like an oryx without the horns,"
Beshte says.

"Is that one new pal," Bunga asks, "or three new pals?"

Unfortunately, the shy okapi is hiding again.
Beshte's friends think Ajabu is imaginary!

The Guard tells Beshte about the leopard. The hippo is worried about his new friend.

"I think I see him!" he says, and runs toward the flamingos' watering hole. All he finds there are flying feathers and surprised squawks.

"Do you think it was the leopard, Beshte?" Kion asks.

"The leopard?" Beshte exclaims. "I thought I saw Ajabu!"

Just then, a deep, angry growl fills the air. The friends turn to see a funny-looking animal with stripes and large ears racing toward them.

"That's Ajabu!" Beshte says happily. "I'm glad you can finally see him."

"The leopard can, too!" Kion says when he notices Makucha running behind the okapi.

Flexing his claws, Makucha leaps toward Ajabu.

"I've got you now!" he snarls.

"Not on my watch!" Beshte says.

WHAM!—the hulking hippo sends Makucha flying through the air. The leopard hits the ground hard.

Makucha continues to battle the hippo, but
the ferocious cat is no match for Beshte!

"Have it your way," Makucha growls as he turns
to run. "No okapi is worth this!"

The Lion Guard is happy to see the leopard go. The animals are also happy to meet Beshte's new, non-imaginary friend, Ajabu!

"You're not planning to go home, are you, Ajabu?" Beshte asks. "That leopard will be there waiting for you."

"What else am I going to do?" Ajabu sighs.

"I think I have an idea!" Kion says with a smile.

"You're welcome to stay in the Pride Lands, Ajabu," Simba says.

"For as long as you like," Nala adds.

"Woo-hoo!" the Lion Guard cheers at the awesome news. Ajabu will never have to hide again—unless he's playing hide-and-seek!